Croatia

JENNIFER HOWSE

MEDIA ENHANCED BOOKS

AV2 BY WEIGL™

ADDED VALUE · AUDIO VISUAL

www.av2books.com

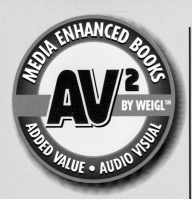

MEDIA ENHANCED BOOKS
AV²
BY WEIGL™
ADDED VALUE • AUDIO VISUAL

AV² provides enriched content that supplements and complements this book. Weigl's AV² books strive to create inspired learning and engage young minds in a total learning experience.

Your AV² Media Enhanced books come alive with...

Audio
Listen to sections of the book read aloud.

Key Words
Study vocabulary, and complete a matching word activity.

Video
Watch informative video clips.

Quizzes
Test your knowledge.

Embedded Weblinks
Gain additional information for research.

Slideshow
View images and captions, and prepare a presentation.

Go to **www.av2books.com**, and enter this book's unique code.

BOOK CODE

AVR96923

Try This!
Complete activities and hands-on experiments.

... and much, much more!

AV² by Weigl brings you media enhanced books that support active learning.

Published by AV² by Weigl
350 5th Avenue, 59th Floor
New York, NY 10118
Website: www.av2books.com

Library of Congress Control Number: 2019938445

ISBN 978-1-7911-0898-4 (hardcover)
ISBN 978-1-7911-0899-1 (softcover)
ISBN 978-1-7911-0900-4 (multi-user eBook)
ISBN 978-1-7911-0901-1 (single-user eBook)

Printed in Guangzhou, China
1 2 3 4 5 6 7 8 9 0 23 22 21 20 19

062019
311018

Editor Heather Kissock
Art Director Terry Paulhus
Layout Tammy West

Photo Credits
Every reasonable effort has been made to trace ownership and to obtain permission to reprint copyright material. The publishers would be pleased to have any errors or omissions brought to their attention so that they may be corrected in subsequent printings.

Weigl acknowledges Getty Images, Alamy, Newscom, iStock, and Shutterstock as its primary photo suppliers for this title.

Contents

Croatia Overview

Located on the northwest part of the Balkan Peninsula, Croatia serves as a gateway to southeastern Europe. Its proximity to the Adriatic Sea provides the country with magnificent coastlines that rise up to mountains in the east and highlands in the north. This dramatic scenery makes Croatia a very popular destination for travelers. While Croatia is now an independent country, this was not always the case. Once part of the former country of Yugoslavia, Croatia had to fight to be its own entity. Today, Croatia's energy, shipbuilding, agriculture, and tourism industries are helping the country gain its footing on the international stage.

Tourists flock to the island of Hvar to rest and relax on its many beaches.

Performing folk dances, such as the moreška, is one way that Croatians keep their traditions alive.

Croatia is known for its truffles. They are used to create a variety of dishes in Croatian restaurants.

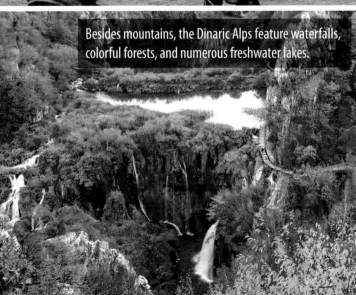
Besides mountains, the Dinaric Alps feature waterfalls, colorful forests, and numerous freshwater lakes.

Ferries run regularly between the Croatian mainland and islands, as well as between the islands themselves.

Exploring Croatia

Croatia covers an area of 21,851 square miles (56,594 square kilometers). The country is separated into 20 individual counties. The Adriatic Sea forms Croatia's western border. Slovenia lies to the country's northwest, while Hungary borders Croatia on the northeast. Serbia neighbors Croatia to the east. Croatia shares a long border with Bosnia and Herzegovina. It winds along the south and southeast part of the country. The southern tip of Croatia sits on the western border of Montenegro.

Zagreb

Krk Island

Italy

N

Tyrrhenian Sea

Lake Vrana

Map Legend

 Croatia

 Land

 Water

 Dinara

Capital City

Krk Island

Lake Vrana

Dinaric Alps

SCALE

250 Miles

250 Kilometers

Krk Island

Croatia has more than 1,000 islands. Krk and the island of Cres are the country's largest islands. Each has an area of 157 square miles (407 sq. km). Krk is the most populated Croatian island. More than 19,000 people live there.

Austria

Hungary

Slovenia

Zagreb

CROATIA

Serbia

Bosnia and
Herzegovina

Dinaric Alps

Adriatic Sea

Dinara

Montenegro

Albania

Lake Vrana

Measuring 12 square miles
(31 sq. km) in area, Vrana is the largest
lake in Croatia. Water from the Adriatic
Sea flows into the lake, so it is both
a freshwater and a saltwater lake.
A variety of birds and fish reside there
as a result.

Zagreb

Zagreb is Croatia's capital and largest city.
More than 807,000 people live there. The
city is divided into three distinct sections.
Upper Town is the oldest part of the city.
Lower Town dates from the 19th century.
New Zagreb is the city's residential area.

Dinara

Dinara is Croatia's highest peak.
Located in the Dinaric Alps, it is
6,004 feet (1,831 meters) above sea
level. Dinara is one of two peaks that
make up Mount Dinara. The other
peak, Troglav, sits on the Bosnia and
Herzegovina side of the mountain.

LAND AND CLIMATE

Croatia is made up of three distinct geographic regions. The Pannonian Plain runs along the north and northeast part of the country. This lowland area is known for its rich soil, fed by the waters of the country's three main rivers, the Sava, Drava, and Danube. Within the Pannonian Plain are several small mountain ranges, including the Papuk Mountains.

Part of the Dinaric Alps, the central mountain belt is located south and west of the Pannonian Plain. A series of cave systems run through the region. It is estimated that this area is home to more than 20,000 caves. Croatia's deepest cave is the Lukina Jama-Trojama, which extends 4,567 feet (1,392 m) underground.

The Zagorje Hills lie on the outskirts of the Pannonian Plain. The area is known for its orchards and vineyards.

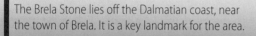

The Brela Stone lies off the Dalmatian coast, near the town of Brela. It is a key landmark for the area.

The Croatian littoral is the country's coastal region. It stretches along the Adriatic coast, extending from the Istrian Peninsula in the north to the Gulf of Kotor in the south—a distance of about 1,100 miles (1,770 km). In between these two points is the region known as Dalmatia. Most of Croatia's islands are located off the Dalmatian coast.

Each of Croatia's geographic regions has its own climate. The Pannonian Plain is warm in the summer and cold in the winter. Summer temperatures average about 75° Fahrenheit (24° Celsius). Winter temperatures average about 59°F (15°C). The central mountain belt has an alpine climate, ranging from 23°F (–5°C) in the winter to 68°F (20°C) in the summer. The Croatian littoral has a Mediterranean climate. This means that it has hot, dry summers and cool, rainy winters. Summer temperatures in this region average about 82°F (28°C). The average winter temperature is about 45°F (7°C). This area can receive up to 60 inches (152 centimeters) of rain per year.

3,626 miles
Total length of Croatia's coastline, including islands. (5,835 km)

26 Number of rivers that flow for more than 30 miles through Croatia. (48 km)

8 Number of national parks in Croatia.

53% Portion of Croatia covered by lowlands.

PLANTS AND ANIMALS

8,582 Number of plant species that grow in Croatia.

1,600 Years Old Age of one of the Mediterranean's oldest olive trees, in Croatia's Brijuni National Park.

151 Number of freshwater fish species swimming in Croatia's waters.

Croatia is rich in **biodiversity**. It has more **species** of plants and animals than most other European countries. Many of these are a result of the varied geography and climate of Croatia. Each region has features that support certain types of organisms.

Plants that are **endemic** to Croatia's islands, for instance, are different from those that grow in the other regions. This is mainly because they developed in isolation on their island home. Endemic island plants include Dubrovnik knapweed, which grows in crevices along coastal cliffs. Plants found in Croatia's mountain areas have to be hardy to survive the alpine climate. The purple Biokovo bellflower is one such plant. It is found only on Biokovo Mountain.

Animals are equally as diverse throughout Croatia. Wolves, bears, and lynxes are three large **mammals** that hunt in the forested mountain areas. Bottlenose dolphins are the country's only resident marine mammal. The olm, a type of salamander, is one of Croatia's eight endemic amphibian species. It lives in the caves of the Dinaric Alps. A bird called the corncrake relies on Croatia's wet grassland areas. The griffon vulture flies along the Adriatic coast.

Croatia has one of Europe's highest populations of Eurasian brown bears. It is estimated that more than 2,500 live in the country's Dinaric Alps.

NATURAL RESOURCES

Croatia's oil and gas reserves are one of the country's most important natural resources. The three main reserves are found southeast of Zagreb, along the Hungarian border, and below the floor of the Adriatic Sea. The country's proven oil reserves total about 70 million barrels.

The country is also realizing the benefits of **renewable energy** sources. Wind farms along the Adriatic coast are helping to supply the country with electricity. Croatia's rivers are used to create **hydroelectricity**. Solar power is now being used to heat homes.

Croatia has about 2 million acres (809,371 hectares) of **arable** land. The varied soil and climate of the regions encourage different agricultural pursuits. These range from vineyards to grain farms.

Croatia's mountains provide resources for the construction industry. Gravel, sand, and construction rocks are all quarried there. Croatia is also known for its salt production. The country has three main salt flats. They are found on Pag Island and in the cities of Ston and Nin.

2004 Year Croatia installed its first wind farm, on Pag Island.

65% Portion of Croatia's energy needs covered by the country's own resources.

2,000 Approximate number of years the city of Ston has been producing salt.

47% Portion of Croatia's total land area covered in forest.

Less than 25 percent of Croatian land is used for agriculture. Most farming takes place in Slavonia, a region in the northeast part of the country.

TOURISM

More than 18 million tourists visit Croatia each year. Some come to see the country's historical sites. Others want to experience the country's many natural areas. The Adriatic's crystal-blue waters and long sandy beaches are a key draw for people looking to relax and have fun in the sun.

Zlatni Rat is a pebble beach that extends about 1,640 feet (500 m) into the sea.

Many international tourists come to Croatia for rest and rejuvenation. Most flock to the country's seaside resorts. Amazing beaches such as the Zlatni Rat, on Brač Island, are ideal for sunbathing and playing beach sports. Other coastal activities offered in Croatia include sailing, fishing, birdwatching, and parasailing around the country's many islands. Those seeking more adventure can take in world-renowned scuba diving. The coastal waters of Croatia provide divers with much to explore, including underwater caves, canyons, pillars, and arches.

Scuba divers can explore several shipwrecks off the coast of Croatia, including the *Baron Gautsch*. This Austrian ship sank in 1914, during World War I, after hitting a mine.

Croatia's coastline offers visitors more than beaches. Coastal cities, such as Dubrovnik and Split, are rich in history and culture. Visitors to Dubrovnik can walk the **ramparts** and imagine what the city would have been like as a fortress in medieval times. In Split, they can spend hours touring the city's ancient Diocletian's Palace, once the home of a Roman emperor. Architecture from the 13th to 16th centuries is on display in Trogir. This medieval walled city, now a **UNESCO** World Heritage Site, was built upon its original Greek and Roman foundations.

The country's inland areas attract tourists who want to experience the great outdoors. A key destination for many tourists is Plitvice Lakes National Park. There, people can walk along pathways and over narrow wooden bridges to see the park's 16 interconnected lakes and more than 90 waterfalls. For those seeking more active pursuits, central Dalmatia is the place to be. Visitors can go whitewater rafting on the Cetina River or glide across the river canyon on a zipline that is almost 500 feet (152 m) above the ground.

Tourism
BY THE NUMBERS

20 feet
Maximum thickness of the walls around Dubrovnik. (6 m)

305^{AD} Year Emperor Diocletian retired to the city of Split.

40 miles per hour
Speed of the zipline ride over Cetina Canyon. (64 km/h)

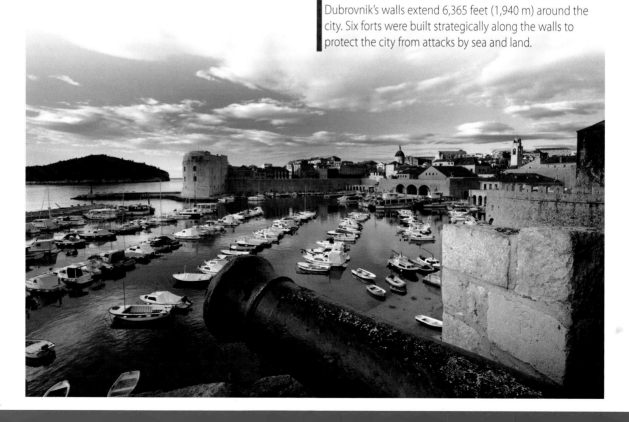

Dubrovnik's walls extend 6,365 feet (1,940 m) around the city. Six forts were built strategically along the walls to protect the city from attacks by sea and land.

INDUSTRY

Manufacturing contributes significantly to Croatia's **economy**, accounting for about 12 percent of the country's **gross domestic product (GDP)**. More than 21,000 businesses are registered as manufacturers in the country. These companies employ a total of approximately 300,000 skilled workers.

The products manufactured in Croatia are wide-ranging. Pharmaceuticals, electronics, and optical products are the country's most technologically advanced sectors. Croatia is also home to companies that produce motor vehicles, machinery, and finished metal products.

Shipbuilding has been important to Croatia since ancient times. The industry flourished well into the 20th century, but has since slowed. Shipbuilders are currently taking steps to modernize their companies and adapt to changing market needs. In the meantime, the future of the industry remains uncertain.

$60.8 Billion Size of Croatia's GDP in 2018.

2nd Croatia's ranking on the list of the most developed countries in the Balkans, after Slovenia.

7,500 Number of workers employed in Croatia's shipbuilding industry.

Located in Split, Brodosplit is Croatia's largest shipyard. Ships have been built here since 1932.

GOODS AND SERVICES

Croatia became a member of the **European Union (EU)** in 2013. Being a member of this organization has helped the country develop trading relationships and improve its economic standing in the world. Croatia **exports** a number of goods. Top exports include mineral-based fuels, machinery, and pharmaceuticals. Italy, Germany, Slovenia, and Bosnia and Herzegovina are Croatia's main customers. Croatia also buys goods from other countries. Some of the products it **imports** include machinery, electrical equipment, and chemicals. Most of these goods come from Italy, Germany, and Slovenia.

Approximately 65 percent of Croatia's workforce is employed in service industries. These workers provide services instead of producing goods. Health care, education, and banking are all service industries. Tourism is a service industry as well. One of the fastest-growing sectors of Croatia's economy, tourism contributes to almost 20 percent of the country's GDP. Seven percent of all workers in Croatia work directly in the tourism industry. They hold jobs such as tour guides and ticket agents.

58.5% Portion of Croatia's GDP represented by the country's service sector.

28 Number of commercial banks in Croatia.

66% Portion of Croatian exports that go to EU countries.

18,000 Number of licenced medical doctors in Croatia.

Oil refineries located along Croatian waterways help to facilitate the easy transfer of the country's oil and gas exports.

INDIGENOUS PEOPLES

Humans have lived in what is now Croatia for at least 40,000 years. Archaeologists have found flints and human remains in various parts of the country. By 3000 BC, several groups had emerged. The Hvar, Danilo, and Impresso cultures built settlements along the Adriatic coast. The Sopot and Korenovo settled farther inland. As the **Bronze Age** took hold, other cultures appeared, including the Vučedol and the Cetina. Ethnic communities began to form during the **Iron Age**, which started in 800 BC. These groups developed trade relations with the peoples of Greece and Italy.

The Romans occupied Croatia from 11 BC to the 5th century AD. Roman buildings such as amphitheaters and forums were built, and people used Roman currency. By the end of the 6th century, however, Roman rule was in decline. **Barbarian** tribes from the north had begun staging raids on the land and its people, pushing the Romans out.

Over time, several **Slavic** groups began to **migrate** to the area. One of these groups was known as the Croats. They settled on the lands that are now Bosnia and Herzegovina and Croatia. By the 8th century, they ruled over the region.

25,000 Number of people the Roman amphitheater in Pula could hold.

3000 BC–1000 AD Years of the Bronze Age.

89.6% Portion of people in Croatia today that identify themselves as Croat.

The Klis Fortress in Dalmatia has a history that is more than 2,000 years old. First occupied by a tribe called the Dalmatae, it later became a Roman stronghold.

CHANGING RULERS

C roatia's location on the Adriatic coast made it a much sought-after territory. During the late 8th and early 9th centuries, Croatia came under the rule of Charlemagne, king of the **Franks**. He organized the Croats into two **principalities**, Dalmatia and Pannonia. However, by the end of the 9th century, Hungary had taken control of Pannonia, and Dalmatia was ruled by a Croatian leader by the name of Tomislav. Over time, he united the two principalities and became Croatia's first king.

Maintaining control of the land was difficult. During the 11th century, the Venetians, **Byzantines**, and Serbs all laid claim to the Croatian coast. The Hungarians reasserted themselves in Pannonia. When the last native Croatian king died in 1097, Hungary's King Coloman claimed the Croatian throne. Upon Coloman's death, the Venetians returned to conquer Dalmatia. They retained control of the area until 1797.

Other parts of Croatia also experienced tumult. The late 1400s saw the **Ottoman Empire** invade from the north. They retained control over much of Croatia until the mid-1600s. This was when the Croats, with the help of Austria's powerful Habsburg family, drove the Ottomans off their land. Now under Habsburg control, the region entered a period of stability.

925
Year Tomislav was crowned Croatia's first king.

1102 Year the Pacta Conventa was signed, uniting Hungary and Croatia politically.

1683–1699 Years of the Great Turkish War, which saw the Ottoman Empire lose most of its European holdings, including Croatia.

Charlemagne became king of the Franks in 771 AD. Nine years later, he was made Holy Roman Emperor by Pope Leo III.

ROAD TO INDEPENDENCE

The early 19th century saw the rise of French emperor Napoleon Bonaparte, who was able to conquer significant portions of Europe. By 1810, his influence stretched from Spain to Austria, and included Austria's Balkan holdings. Napoleon grouped Croatia and its surrounding lands into an area he called the Illyrian Provinces. He then took steps to bring improvements to the region. A tree-planting program restored vegetation to the mountainsides. Schools, hospitals, and roads were built. New agricultural programs were put in place.

Napoleon sent Auguste de Marmont to his newly formed Illyria Provinces to govern them on his behalf. Marmont was stationed in the area from 1805 to 1810.

The Napoleonic Empire fell in 1815. The land now known as Croatia came under Austria's control, with much of it being governed by Austria's Hungarian province. After years of being united as Illyria, the people were not pleased to be separated. A **nationalist** movement began. Its goals were to join the individual provinces into one nation and to establish a common language. The movement had minimal success, and ultimately, the lands of Illyria became part of the **Austro-Hungarian Empire**.

Napoleon gained his Croatian land following the 1809 Battle of Wagram against Austria.

The Austro-Hungarian Empire fell during World War I, leaving its holdings in a state of disarray. Croatia signed an agreement to unite with the countries of Serbia and Slovenia. By 1929, the three countries were known as the Kingdom of Yugoslavia. Croatia remained one of six **republics** within Yugoslavia for 62 years.

During World War II, Yugoslavia was occupied by Germany, and in the post-war years, it was part of the **Soviet Union**. Following the war, Yugoslavia's leader was Josip Broz Tito. He was able to keep the region together. However, when he died in 1980, tensions rose between the different republics. On June 25, 1991, the people of Croatia voted for independence. The EU and the **United Nations** recognized Croatia as a country in its own right the following year.

Croatia's declaration of independence led other Yugoslavian republics to do the same. This led to a civil war that lasted for 10 years, from 1991 to 2001.

1.5 million
Population of the Illyrian Provinces in 1811.

93%
Portion of the Croatian population that voted for independence in 1991.

20,000
Approximate number of people who died during the Croatian War of Independence.

POPULATION

More than 4.1 million people live in Croatia. The majority live in the northern part of the country. In fact, one quarter of the country's total population live in and around the capital of Zagreb. The population of Zagreb itself is approximately 807,000. Split, the country's second-largest city, has a population of about 180,000. The island populations are sparse.

Croatia has an older population. The largest segment of the population, about 55 percent, is aged between 25 and 64 years old. Another 19 percent is over the age of 65. This imbalance is creating a problem in Croatia as the population is not replenishing itself. Instead, younger people are moving to developed countries for better employment opportunities. Based on current trends, it is estimated that Croatia's population will be reduced to about 3.1 million people by 2050. It is currently ranked as the world's 14th fastest-shrinking country.

42.9 Median age in Croatia.

80 Number of people per square mile in Croatia. (2.6 sq. km)

57% Portion of Croatians living in the country's urban centers.

In 2017, only 28.7 percent of Croatians aged 30 to 34 had university degrees. The University of Zagreb is the largest university in the country, with approximately 72,500 students.

POLITICS AND GOVERNMENT

Today, the government of Croatia operates as a **parliamentary republic**. Croatia's head of state is the president. He or she represents Croatia on the world stage and chooses the prime minister. It is the prime minister's job to lead the government. The president is chosen by the people of Croatia in elections held every five years. The prime minister is typically the leader of the political party that holds the majority of seats in Parliament. He or she is responsible for forming a cabinet. Each cabinet member is given his or her own department to run.

Croatia has a **unicameral** parliament. Called the Sabor, it is responsible for the proposal, debate, and approval of any legislation facing the country. The Sabor has 151 seats. Its members are elected, with elections held every four years. Most members are elected based on political party affiliations. However, eight seats are reserved for representatives of Croatia's minorities. These members are elected solely by the minority they represent.

Upholding the country's laws is the job of Croatia's court system. The Supreme Court is made up of a president, vice-president, and 41 justices. The country also has county, municipal, and commercial court systems.

1273 Year of the first recorded sitting of the Sabor.

50.7% Portion of votes Kolinda Grabar-Kitarović received in 2015 to become the country's first female president.

16 Voting age for employed Croatians, with all others allowed to vote at age 18.

Croatia's Parliament building is located at St. Mark's Square in Zagreb. Construction on the building began in 1731. It was completed in 1737.

CULTURAL GROUPS

T he Croats are the largest ethnic group living in Croatia and make up most of the population. Their cultural traditions, folklore, and language contribute significantly to the country's identity. There is, however, much diversity within Croatian culture. This is partly because the country and its people have been influenced by the many groups and nations that occupied it. Regional influences have also helped to create various subgroups within Croatian culture.

Lacemaking has been a tradition in Croatia for centuries. Today, it continues to be passed down from one generation to the next.

While Croatia is a modern country, it does much to keep its traditions alive. Groups dedicated to Croatian music, dance, and crafts can be found throughout the land. Several folklore festivals are held every year. One of the best known is the Zagreb International Folklore Festival. Held every July, the festival celebrates the folklore of Croatia's many regions. People might see a performance of the Lindo, a Croatian dance with a Spanish influence. They may also hear a musician play the lijerica, an instrument similar to a violin, or a vocal group sing in the koleda style.

Besides performances, the Zagreb International Folklore Festival also features workshops, exhibitions, and craft displays.

The Croatian language can be heard at folklore festivals and in the country's many cities and towns. Three **dialects** of Croatian are spoken. The Štokavian dialect is the most widespread, found mainly in the country's south and east. Most people living in the northern part of the country use the Kajkavian dialect. The Čakavian dialect can be heard mostly along the Adriatic coast. The languages of the country's minority groups can also be heard in various parts of the country. These languages include Serbian, Italian, and Czech.

Religion plays an important role in Croatian culture. While under Soviet control, religious practices in the country were discouraged. Today, however, most of the population is involved in some form of religion. Currently, 91 percent of the population identify themselves as Christians. Most of these people are Roman Catholics. The Catholic influence can be seen throughout the country, with the church being a key structure in every community. Most communities also have their own patron saint. Other religions practiced in Croatia include Eastern Orthodox, Protestantism, and Islam.

6,000 Approximate number of Czechs living in Croatia.

86.3% Portion of Croatian population that is Roman Catholic.

1966 Year the first Zagreb International Folklore Festival was held.

The importance of religion to Croatians throughout history can be seen in the detailed work inside the country's churches, including Križevci Cathedral, in the northern part of the country.

ARTS AND ENTERTAINMENT

The arts have flourished in Croatia for centuries. As early as 2000 BC, people were making art a part of their everyday lives. One of the earliest examples of Croatian art is the Vučedol Dove. On display at the Archaeological Museum in Zagreb, this ceramic drinking vessel was made by the Vučedol people more than 4,000 years ago. Artistic creation has continued to be an integral part of Croatian life ever since.

The Vučedol Dove was found in 1938 during an archaeological dig.

The country has produced a variety of artists over the years. Andrija Buvina was an important sculptor in the Middle Ages. He is best known for carving the wooden doors at the Cathedral of Saint Domnius, in Split. One of Croatia's best-known painters is Vlaho Bukovac. Born in the 1800s in the village of Cavtat, he went to Paris to train in the **Impressionist** style. Twentieth-century painter Edo Murtić explored themes of war, fear, and suffering. Following Murtić's death, his family donated 1,500 of his works to the City of Zagreb.

Vlaho Bukovac's home in Cavtat is now a museum devoted to his life and work. Many of his paintings are on display, including a self-portrait of the artist with his family.

Some of the earliest samples of Croatian literature are in the form of illuminated manuscripts. Dating from the 11th century, these religious texts have pictures painted in the margins that bring the words to life. Marko Marulić was also creating works at this time. Mainly a poet, Marulić is also known as the first person to use the word "psychology" in a written work. The late 19th century saw writers such as Evgenij Kumičić and Ksaver Šandor Gjalski draw attention to the lives of the country's lower classes. Croatia's literary tradition continues today with writers such as Zoran Ferić and Julijana Matanović.

Croatia has been producing movies since 1917. Its first full-length feature film with sound, *Lisinski*, was released in 1944. Today, one of Croatia's most successful actors is Goran Visnjic. Born in Sibenik in 1972, Visnjic began acting as a child. He found success in the United States when he starred on the medical drama *ER*. Since then, he has been in demand as an actor, starring in the 2011 movie *The Girl with the Dragon Tattoo* and the television series *Santa Clarita Diet*.

1989 Year Croatian pop group Riva won the Eurovision Song Contest.

13,000 Number of Croatian sculptures in the Glyptotheque Zagreb museum's collection.

60 Number of professional theaters in Croatia.

Goran Visnjic starred on *ER* from 1999 to 2008.

SPORTS

Croatia is a sporting nation. Not only do Croatians enjoy watching and participating in sports played around the world, they are also involved in sports unique to their country. One such sport is picigin. First developed in Split, picigin is a ball game that has its roots in water polo. It is typically played in ankle-level water with five players. The object of the game is to ensure the small ball does not touch the water. Picigin players use a variety of techniques to pass the ball to each other. Besides passing and hitting, they also perform leaps and other acrobatic moves. The game is not competitive. All players work to keep the ball in the air.

Picigin is believed to have been developed by university students in 1908.

Another ball game popular in Croatia is far more competitive. Soccer is one of the most-watched sports in the country, and the national team works hard not to disappoint. Historically, the Croatian team has had very strong showings at the World Cup. One of its best results was in 1998, when the team finished in third place. This was topped, however, at the 2018 World Cup, when Croatia finished second over all.

Croatia's national soccer team has been competing since 1993, shortly after the country declared independence.

Croatia has also produced a number of top-rated tennis players. Marin Čilić has won 18 Association of Tennis Professionals (ATP) Championships, including the 2014 U.S. Open. Čilić won the U.S. Open with the help of his coach, Goran Ivanišević. A player in his own right, Ivanišević won the Wimbledon men's championship in 2001.

In 1992, Croatia took part in its first Olympic Games as an independent nation. Croatian athletes have since gone on to acquire numerous Olympic medals. One of the greatest athletes in Croatia is Olympian Blanka Vlašić. At the 2008 Olympic Games, Blanka won the silver medal in the high jump. Alpine skier Janica Kostelić has raced to four Olympic gold medals. She won her first three golds in 2002, becoming the only woman to win three alpine skiing golds in a single Olympics. Her fourth gold was won in 2006. Croatia has also done well in Olympic team sports. The country's handball team won the gold medal in 1996 and 2004. Its water polo team won gold in 2012.

Marin Čilić began playing tennis at the age of seven. He joined the professional ranks in 2005.

10 Number of Olympic medals Croatia has won in alpine skiing.

1909 Year Franjo Bučar founded the Croatia Sports Federation.

16,000 Number of sports associations operating in Croatia.

Mapping Croatia

We use many tools to interpret maps and to understand the locations of features such as cities, states, lakes, and rivers. The map below has many tools to help interpret information on Croatia.

Map of Croatia

★ Zagreb

45°N

Pula •

Zadar •

Adriatic Sea

▲ Dinara

Lake Vrana

Trogir • • Split

Dubrovnik •

15°E   20°E

40°N

MAP LEGEND

★ Capital City
• City
🌀 Body of Water
🍃 Lake
-·-·- Country Border
▲ Mountain
╲ Longitude & Latitude
⬜ Croatia
⬜ Other Countries

N
W   E
S

SCALE
0   150 Miles
0   150 Kilometers

Mapping Tools

- The compass rose shows north, south, east, and west. The points in-between represent northeast, northwest, southeast, and southwest.

- The map scale shows that the distances on a map represent much longer distances in real life. If you measure the distance between objects on a map, you can use the map scale to calculate the actual distance in miles or kilometers between those two points.

- The lines of latitude and longitude are long lines that appear on maps. The lines of latitude run east to west and measure how far north or south of the equator a place is located. The lines of longitude run north to south and measure how far east or west of the Prime Meridian a place is located. A location on a map can be found by using the two numbers where latitude and longitude meet. This number is called a coordinate and is written using degrees and direction. For example, the city of Zagreb would be found at 46°N and 16°E on a map.

Map It!

Using the map and the appropriate tools, complete the activities below.

Locating with latitude and longitude
1. Which city is located at 42°N and 18°E?
2. Which mountain is located at 44°N and 16°E?
3. Which lake is found at 44°N and 15°E?

Distances between points
4. Using the map scale and a ruler, calculate the approximate distance between Split and Trogir.
5. Using the map scale and a ruler, calculate the approximate distance between Zagreb and Dubrovnik.
6. Using the map scale and a ruler, calculate the approximate distance between Zadar and Pula.

ANSWERS 1. Dubrovnik 2. Dinara 3. Lake Vrana 4. 18 miles (29 km) 5. 241 miles (388 km) 6. 86 miles (138 km)

Quiz Time

Test your knowledge of Croatia by answering these questions.

1 What nation was Croatia part of between 1929 and 1991?

2 What body of water forms Croatia's western border?

3 What is Croatia's highest peak?

4 Where does the olm live?

5 What is Croatia's parliament called?

6 How many tourists visit Croatia each year?

7 How many dialects does the Croatian language have?

8 What is the population of Zagreb?

9 What was the GDP of Croatia in 2018?

10 What traditional sport was developed in Split?

ANSWERS

1. Yugoslavia
2. Adriatic Sea
3. Dinara
4. In the caves of the Dinaric Alps
5. Sabor
6. More than 18 million
7. Three
8. More than 807,000
9. $60.8 billion
10. Picigin

Key Words

arable: suitable for growing crops

Austro-Hungarian Empire: the dual monarchy established in 1867 that saw Austria and Hungary share the same ruler

barbarian: a person from a country that is considered inferior

biodiversity: the range of living organisms within an area

Bronze Age: a prehistoric period that saw weapons and tools made of bronze instead of stone

Byzantines: people of the Eastern Roman Empire

dialects: regional varieties of the same language

economy: the production, distribution, and consumption of goods and services

endemic: native and restricted to a certain place

European Union (EU): a political and economic organization, established in 1993, that has more than two dozen member countries

exports: sells to other countries

Franks: a group of Germanic peoples

gross domestic product (GDP): the total value of goods and services produced in a country or area

hydroelectricity: electricity produced using the energy of moving water, such as in a river

imports: buys from other countries

Impressionist: a style of art that focuses on the effects of light on an object

Iron Age: a prehistoric age that saw weapons and tools made of iron instead of bronze

mammals: animals that have hair or fur and drink their mother's milk

median age: the age that divides a population into two numerically equal groups

migrate: to go from one region to another

nationalist: a person who is devoted to his or her country

Ottoman Empire: Turkish rulers that controlled Eastern Europe between the 14th and 20th centuries

parliamentary republic: a country that has a largely ceremonial head of state and is run by an elected head of government

peninsula: a land mass that extends out into a body of water

principalities: states ruled by princes

ramparts: defensive walls

renewable energy: electricity and other forms of energy produced from resources that will not be used up over time, such as sunlight, wind, or flowing water in rivers

republics: in the Soviet Union, states in which the government is formed by workers' councils and based on Soviet democracy

Slavic: relating to people from parts of Eastern Europe

Soviet Union: a former country in eastern Europe and Asia

species: groups of organisms that share similar features

UNESCO: United Nations Educational, Scientific and Cultural Organization, whose main goals are to promote world peace and eliminate poverty through education, science, and culture

unicameral: having a single legislative chamber

United Nations: an international organization founded in 1945 to promote peace and cooperation among nations

Index

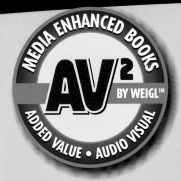

Log on to www.av2books.com

AV² by Weigl brings you media enhanced books that support active learning. Go to www.av2books.com, and enter the special code found on page 2 of this book. You will gain access to enriched and enhanced content that supplements and complements this book. Content includes video, audio, weblinks, quizzes, a slideshow, and activities.

AV² Online Navigation

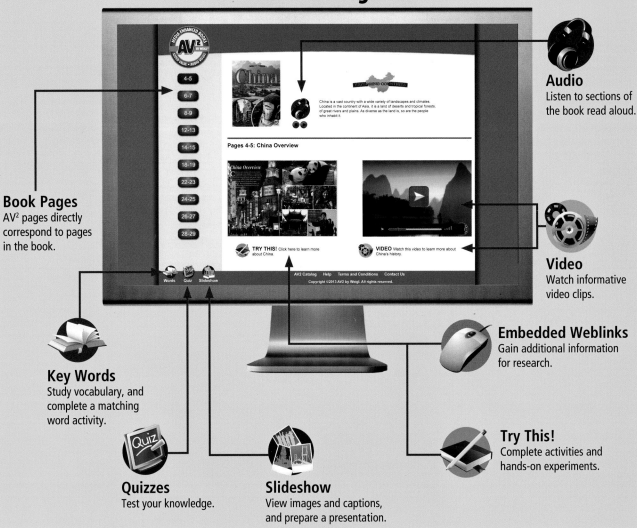

Audio
Listen to sections of the book read aloud.

Book Pages
AV² pages directly correspond to pages in the book.

Video
Watch informative video clips.

Key Words
Study vocabulary, and complete a matching word activity.

Embedded Weblinks
Gain additional information for research.

Quizzes
Test your knowledge.

Slideshow
View images and captions, and prepare a presentation.

Try This!
Complete activities and hands-on experiments.

AV² was built to bridge the gap between print and digital. We encourage you to tell us what you like and what you want to see in the future.

Sign up to be an AV² Ambassador at www.av2books.com/ambassador.

Due to the dynamic nature of the internet, some of the URLs and activities provided as part of AV² by Weigl may have changed or ceased to exist. AV² by Weigl accepts no responsibility for any such changes. All media enhanced books are regularly monitored to update addresses and sites in a timely manner. Contact AV² by Weigl at 1-866-649-3445 or av2books@weigl.com with any questions, comments, or feedback.